Roary's First Day

First published in Great Britain by HarperCollins Children's Books in 2007

10 9 8 7 6 5 4 3

ISBN-10: 0-00-725305-2   ISBN-13: 978-0-00-725305-0

© Chapman Entertainment Limited & David Jenkins 2007

A CIP catalogue record for this title is available from the British Library.

Based on the television series Roary the Racing Car and the original script
'Roary's First Day' by Rachel Dawson.
© Chapman Entertainment Limited & David Jenkins 2007

Visit Roary at: www.roarytheracingcar.com

Printed and bound in Italy by LEGO

Roary's First Day

HarperCollins *Children's Books*

It had been a busy day at Silver Hatch racetrack. Big Chris and Marsha were getting everything ready for a big race the next day.

"Cars all checked?" Marsha asked.

"Yep, all done," Big Chris nodded. "Don't worry Marsha, everything's ready for the big race tomorrow."

"Great, I'm off home then!" said Marsha.

"Phew, what a day," said Big Chris. Just as he was about to lock up the garage, he heard a strange revving noise inside.

In the workshop, all the cars were happily fast asleep.
All the cars except for one.
Over in the furthest bay, Big Chris spotted Roary, revving
and shaking in his sleep.
"Ahh!" yelled Roary, waking with a start. "Big Chris!
I crashed in the middle of the big race!"
"It's okay, Roary," Big Chris gently patted his bonnet to
try and calm him down. "You just had a bad dream."

"I can't race tomorrow, Big Chris," Roary said nervously.
"I'm scared I'll mess it up, just like in my dream!"
"No you won't, Roary," smiled Big Chris. "How's about I tell
you a story to help you get back to sleep?"
"Yes, please," giggled Roary, settling back down.
"Okay, so it was Roary's very first day in Silver Hatch..."
Big Chris began.

Roary began to fall back to sleep as Big Chris told his story...
"He's a great little car, Mr Carburettor," Marsha said, proudly.
"Yes, not in the same league as my Maxi," Mr Carburettor said.
"But he has potential. Welcome to Silver Hatch, Roary."
Roary watched the other cars dash around the track. "Wow, I'll never be able to do that."
"Of course you will!" came a little voice behind him. Roary span around to see a little pink stunt car, smiling at him.

"I'm Cici," she said. "And you must be Roary."

"Y-y-yes," Roary stuttered. She was very pretty. "Er, do you race too?"

"Yes and so will you," she said. "I'm off to do some practise laps but I'll be back to see how you are later. Au revoir!"

She zoomed off around the track, leaving Roary to stare after her.

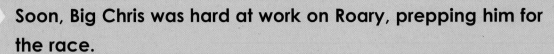

Soon, Big Chris was hard at work on Roary, prepping him for the race.

"Welcome to your new home, Roary," he said. "This is where my number one star will sleep!"

Roary smiled. "Your number one star? Oh, thanks, Big Chris!"

Big Chris gave him a big grin in return and started playing with his engine.

"Ooh, that **tickles!**" laughed Roary.

"Hey, Chris!" someone shouted angrily across the workshop.
"When are you going to stop tinkering with that squirt?
My oil needs topping up!"

"Hey, Maxi," scolded Big Chris. "That's no way to
welcome Roary!"

"Sorry," Maxi said quietly and rolled away.

"Pay no attention to him," Big Chris whispered to Roary,
"he doesn't mean any harm."

In no time at all, Roary was ready to test out his engine. "Hello, Roary," called Cici. "How's it going, Big Chris?"

"I'm all done with Roary," Big Chris said, "why don't you show him around?"

"Love to!" grinned Cici. "How are you settling in?"

"I don't think I belong here," Roary said sadly as they rolled out on to the track. "I'm not a proper racing car."

"You look like one to me!" Cici said. "Come on, I'll show you around Silver Hatch."

"This is Rusty," she said, pointing towards a large, old-looking caravan, "where Big Chris lives."

"Keep the noise down!" Rusty muttered, opening one eye.

"Oh, you must be the new arrival, sorry, just getting my beauty sleep."

Roary looked over at Cici and giggled.

"That's the starter's grid, and the commentary tower," Cici said, pointing out all of Silver Hatch's landmarks. "Now I'll show you the rest of the track – race you!" Cici raced off and without even thinking about it, Roary tore off after her as fast as he could. The rest of the cars were revving their engines on the starter's grid for a practise lap as the two little cars appeared on the horizon.

"Okay," Big Chris said to Maxi, Drifter and Tin Top as they lined up. "I want you to do one last practise lap to check your engines are running smoothly."

As the flag went down, they set off with roaring engines and whizzing tyres, quickly followed by Roary and Cici!
"That's my boy," smiled Big Chris.

As all the cars whirled around the race track, Roary was having so much fun, he didn't even know he was in a race!

He whizzed passed Cici, dodged by Drifter and overtook Tin Top without a second glance.

Before he knew where he was, Roary was locked in a bumper-to-bumper battle with Maxi, the fastest car in all of Silver Hatch, for first place!

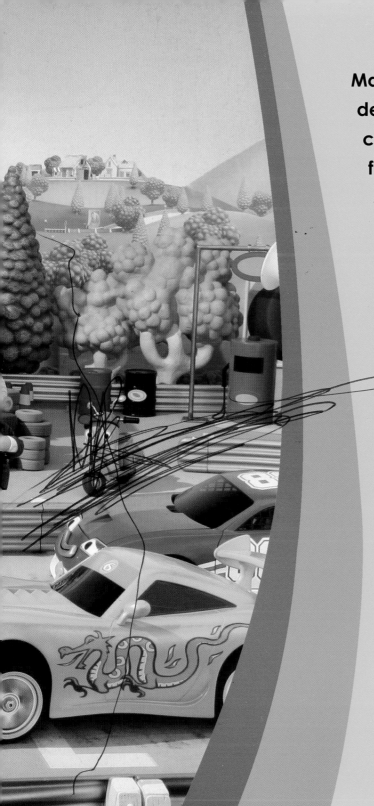

Maxi snarled and pushed ahead, determined to beat the little red race car but Roary was too excited. As the finishing line appeared, Roary **zoomed** into the lead. He had won the race!

"Wow," said Roary. "Maybe I can be a real racing car after all..."

"...and he was the best little racing car in all of Silver Hatch," said Big Chris, finishing the story. Roary snored happily now, fast asleep. "I think that story did the trick!" Big Chris smiled. "Good night, Roary. Sleep tight."

The next morning, Roary woke bright and early, all excited about the big race. "Morning everyone!" he called out to the other cars. "Ready for the big race?"

"Mamma mia," groaned Maxi, "I have to be perfect. My oil, my oil…"

"My tyres feel flat," said Drifter. "I won't be able to glide around corners!"

"What if I don't beat my lap time?" fretted Cici.

"I just know I'm gonna crash!" moaned Tin Top.

"Don't worry everyone!" said Roary cheerfully. "It's okay to be nervous. Maybe I can tell you a story about a brave little red racing car?"

And so Roary told the others how he overcame his nerves on his first day at Silver Hatch. The other cars forgot all their worries and even began to look forward to the big race!

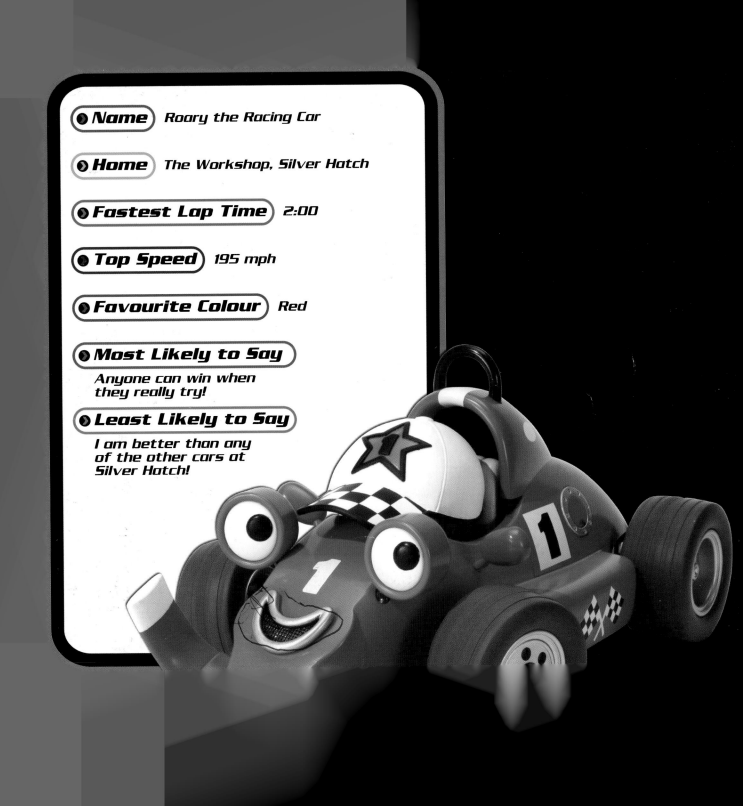

- **Name** Roary the Racing Car
- **Home** The Workshop, Silver Hatch
- **Fastest Lap Time** 2:00
- **Top Speed** 195 mph
- **Favourite Colour** Red
- **Most Likely to Say**

  Anyone can win when they really try!

- **Least Likely to Say**

  I am better than any of the other cars at Silver Hatch!

Roary